Draw with Me!

A GOLDEN BOOK • NEW YORK

ISBN: 978-0-375-86604-3
www.randomhouse.com/kids
Printed in the United States of America
10 9 8 7 6 5 4 3 2 1

**Ni hao! I'm Kai-lan.
What's your name?**

The pictures in this book need to be finished. Will you help? Super!

Where is Mr. Sun?
Will you draw him?

Let's tickle Mr. Sun.
Will you draw a smile on him?

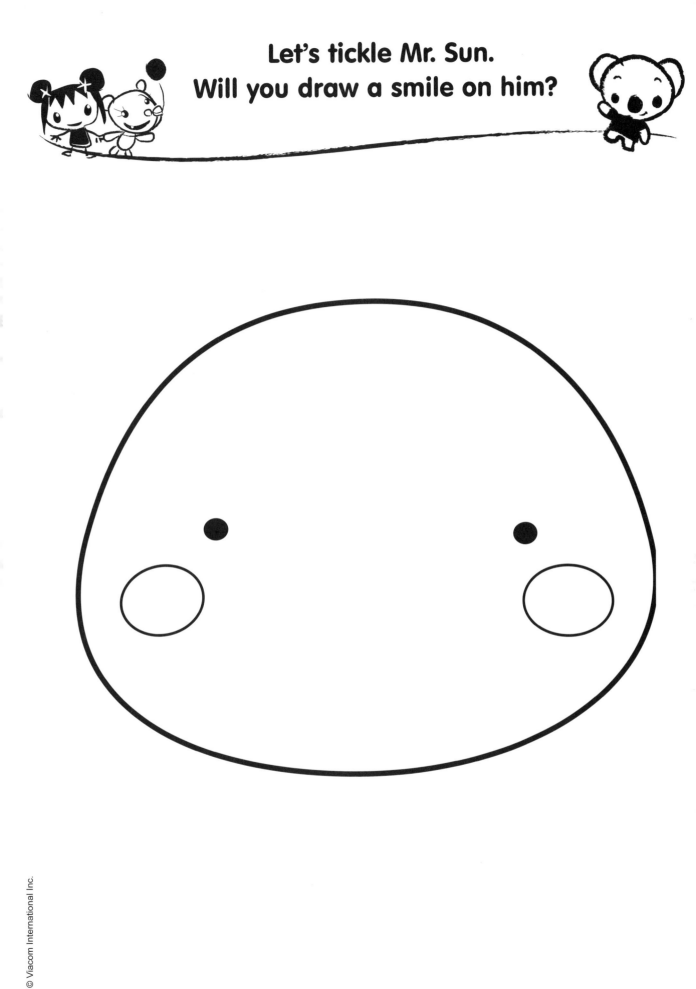

Sun fuzzies tickle.
Will you draw some more?

I like putting flowers in my hair.
Will you draw some for me?

Will you draw some hearts on my shirt?

Tolee is sliding down to see me. Will you finish drawing the bamboo?

Draw Pandy on Tolee's shirt.

**Tolee and Hoho are super happy
to see each other!
Will you draw their smiles?**

Will you draw a big pile of leaves for Hoho and Tolee to jump in?

Where is Rintoo's tooth?
Will you draw it for him?

Will you draw a ball
for Rintoo to balance on?

Will you draw a path so Rintoo can get home?

That's Rintoo's house.
Finish the roof for him.

Will you help Rintoo decorate
the sign on his house?
Draw another paw print on it.

Do you like my flower?
Draw one for yourself.

Will you draw
a balloon for Lulu?

Where are YeYe's glasses?
Will you draw them?

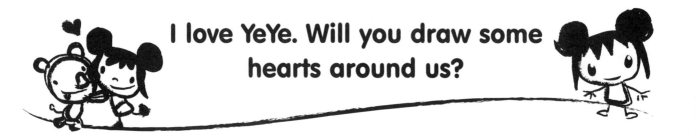

I love YeYe. Will you draw some hearts around us?

YeYe has an awesome garden. Will you draw some vegetables growing in it?

I have YeYe's watering can.
Will you draw a rake
and a shovel?

Will you draw the tallest flower in YeYe's garden?

Now draw the shortest flower in the garden.

Will you draw apples in YeYe's tree?

Fill YeYe's basket with apples.

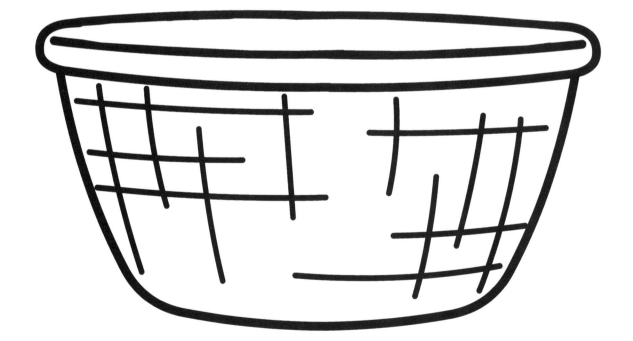

Tiao! That's how I say *jump* in Chinese. Will you draw Hoho jumping over me?

Will you draw a twirly whirly flower for me to catch?

The flower landed
on YeYe's head.
Will you draw it?

We're having a Lantern Festival.
What is Rintoo painting
on his lantern?

Decorate your own lantern.

What did Hoho draw on his lantern?

Will you draw an apple
on top of Tolee's lantern
so it won't blow away?

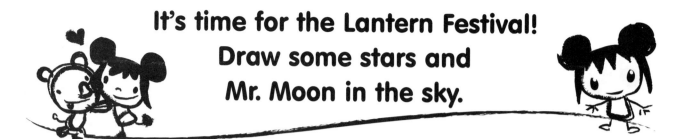

It's time for the Lantern Festival!
Draw some stars and
Mr. Moon in the sky.

The fireflies are here to light up our lanterns. Will you draw more fireflies?

Will you draw lanterns on our bamboo poles?

Will you draw a path so I can get to my house?

**Will you draw stairs
so I can visit Rintoo?**

Draw a super special picture here!

I love my heart-box purse.
Will you finish it for me?

I love dinosaurs. Will you draw a balloon shaped like a dinosaur for me?

I love playing in the park with my friends. Will you draw a jump rope for us?

It's a windy day.
Will you draw a kite for Tolee?

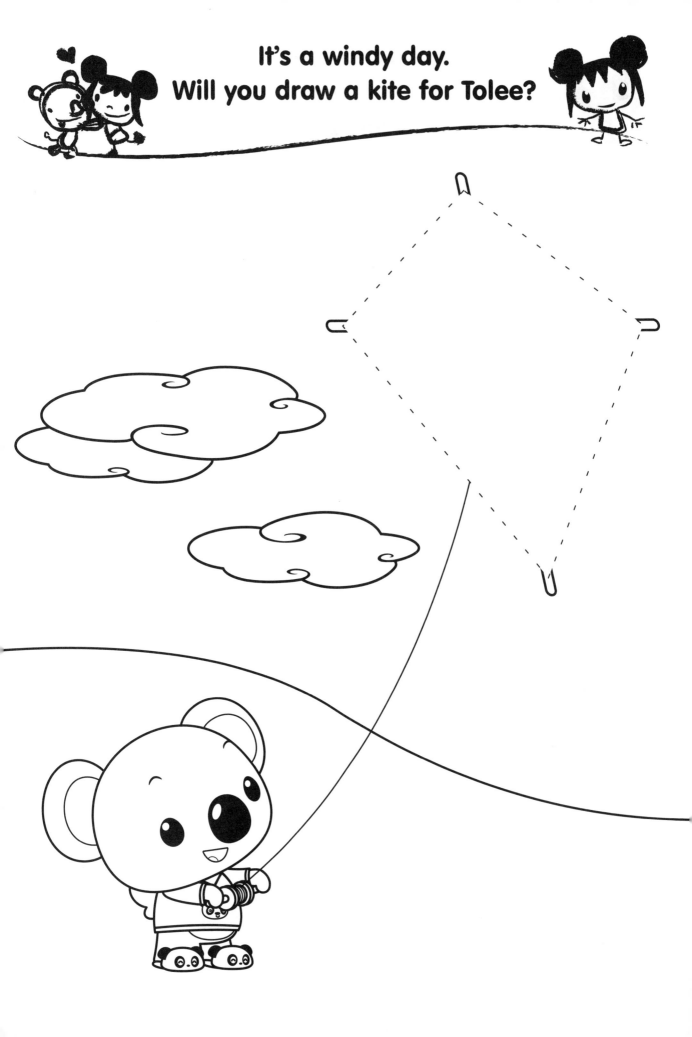

YeYe brought us a treat!
Will you draw the
picnic basket?

Let's have a picnic. Will you draw a blanket for us?

Draw a snack for Hoho.
Color it red. *Hong se!*

Will you draw
a bird in the sky?

Will you draw a trampoline for us to jump on?

Will you draw a flower for me to smell?

Will you draw a wheel on my bike?

We're making a big pile of flowers. Will you draw more flowers for us to collect?

Hoho likes throwing leaves.
Will you draw more
leaves in the air?

What is Hoho jumping over?

Our friends the ants are building a bridge. Will you draw some wood for the crane to lift?

Will you help the ants finish building the bridge?

Will you draw a twirly whirly flower for the ant to ride on?

Will you fill this tree with pretty flowers?

Here comes Rintoo.
Will you finish his big balloon?

**Tolee wants a balloon shaped
like a giant panda.
Will you draw one for him?**

Will you draw
a friend for this frog?

Hua! That's how I say *flower* in Chinese. Will you draw a flower for this bee to smell?

I like to play my tambourine.
Draw an instrument you like to play.

Where's my other shoe?
Will you draw it for me?

Hoho wants to roller-skate. Will you draw wheels for him?

Rintoo's car needs wheels to make it go, go, go!

We're having a race. Will you draw a finish line for us?

Will you draw a tennis racket for Rintoo?

Now we need a net.
Will you draw one for us?

Oh, no! It's starting to rain.
Draw some clouds and rain.

Will you draw an umbrella for me?

Hoho loves jumping in puddles. Will you draw a big puddle for him?

What a super day!
Will you draw a rainbow
in the sky?

Our boat needs a sail.
Will you help us draw it?

I love playing at the beach.
Will you draw my pail?

**Tolee wants to build
a super sand castle.
Will you help him?**

Will you draw a big towel for Rintoo and a small one for Hoho?

 **Will you draw a ball for me to throw to Hoho?**

Will you draw a wave for Rintoo to surf on?

We're collecting seashells.
Will you draw some for us?

It's time for the Dragon Boat Race! Help YeYe decorate his boat.

Rintoo is putting on his awesome racing helmet. Will you finish it for him?

Will you draw another belt on Hoho's vest so he'll be super safe?

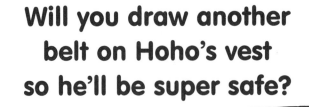

Who is in the boat?

Rintoo and I are in a boat race. Will you finish drawing our paddles?

Draw some waves around Lulu and Hoho's boat.

**Oh, no! Rintoo lost the race.
How do you think he feels?**

The Hula Ducks will make Rintoo
feel better. Draw another Hula
Duck, and a smile on Rintoo.

Draw yourself with the Hula Ducks.

Hoho is very relaxed.
What is he thinking about?

**We can meet Mr. Dragon
at the end of the race!
Draw him.**

Will you color this flower for Mr. Dragon?

KEY
1=PINK 2=YELLOW 3=GREEN

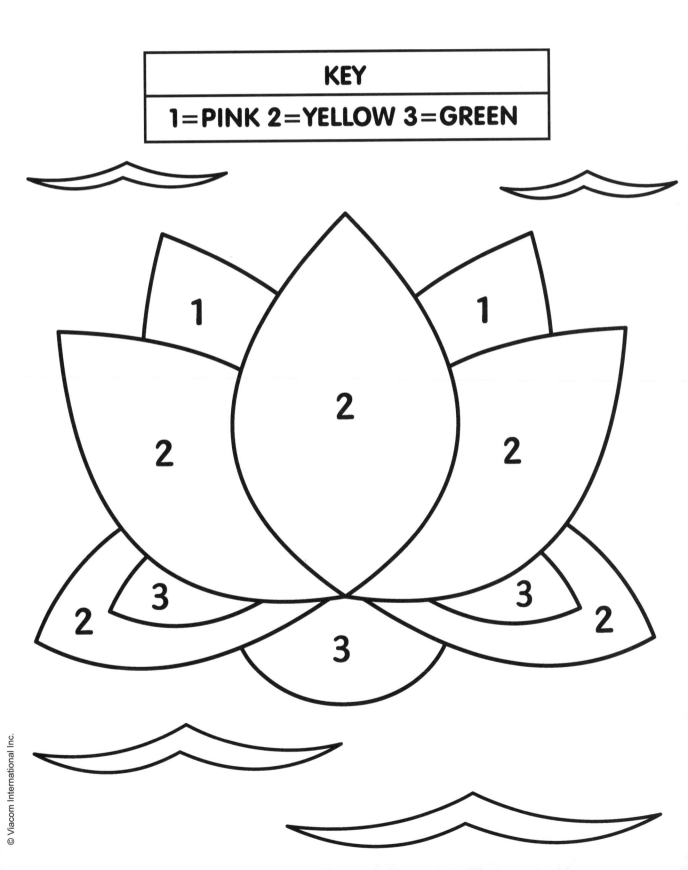

Draw some fish in the pond.

Let's go on a safari.
Will you finish
drawing our hats?

We're looking for our friend Stompy the Elephant. Will you finish drawing his trunk?

Will you draw apples for Stompy?

Will you draw some grass for Rintoo to run through? Color it green. *Lu se!*

Will you draw a hat for the Peeking Mouse?

We're drawing pictures of our favorite things. Will you draw your favorite thing for us?

**Rintoo can't wait
for our Super Party.
What will he bring?**

YeYe is thinking of the snack
he'll make for the party.
What do you think it is?

Let's decorate for the party. Will you draw some balloons and add some lanterns?

Will you draw party hats on Rintoo and Tolee?

Mr. Fluffy baked a special treat for the party. What do you think it is?

Here come Lulu and Howard.
Will you draw some clouds around them?

Will you finish
the heart for me?

Hoho loves to spin his turntables.
Draw yourself dancing
to Hoho's music.

Will you finish
DJ Hoho's headphones?

Let's have a sleepover.
Will you decorate my pajamas?

Let's play in my room.
Draw your favorite toys.

I really like dinosaur toys. Will you draw some more?

What's on your pajamas? Use your crayons and decorate the pajamas.

YeYe is putting up a tent
for our sleepover.
Will you draw it for us?

**The fireflies will make sure
it's not too dark in the tent.
Will you draw some more?**

Will you draw
some slippers for me?

Will you decorate my sleeping bag?

I need a backpack for the sleepover.
Will you decorate it?

Will you draw the number 1 on Rintoo's shirt?

**Rintoo likes his yummy snack.
Will you draw a big
smile on his face?**

We're making silly faces.
Will you draw your funny face here?

Will you decorate my ladybug tent with polka dots?

**Hoho wants a banana
on his pajamas.
Will you draw one?**

Shhh. Hoho is sleeping. Will you decorate his sleeping bag?

You make my heart feel super happy! Will you draw some hearts in the air?